W9-AHQ-141

DATE DUE	
AUG 3 1 2001	
DEC 2 0 2001	
JUL - 3 2003	
GAYLORD	PRINTED IN U.S.A.

This book was purchased with funds provided through a grant from the State of Louisiana.

A CAJUN TALL TALE

Feliciana
Meets d'Loup Garou

by
Tynia Thomassie

Illustrated by
Cat Bowman Smith

Little, Brown and Company
Boston   New York   Toronto   London

ST. JOHN THE BAPTIST PARISH LIBRARY
1334 WEST AIRLINE HIGHWAY
LaPLACE, LOUISIANA 70068

For my boys, Matthew and Will, who can drive their Memère
to the brink, and pull her back again with a smile
T. T.

For Anna and the little one
C. B. S.

Text copyright © 1998 by Tynia Thomassie
Illustrations copyright © 1998 by Cat Bowman Smith

All rights reserved. No part of this book may be reproduced in any form or
by any electronic or mechanical means, including information storage and
retrieval systems, without permission in writing from the publisher, except
by a reviewer who may quote brief passages in a review.

First Edition

Library of Congress Cataloging-in-Publication Data

Thomassie, Tynia.
    Feliciana meets d'Loup Garou : a Cajun tall tale / by Tynia Thomassie ;
illustrated by Cat Bowman Smith — 1st ed.
        p.   cm.
    Summary: Spunky Feliciana Feydra LeRoux outsmarts the
Cajun boogeyman who pays nighttime visits to misbehaving children.
    ISBN 0-316-84133-1
    [1. Behavior — Fiction.   2. Monsters — Fiction.   3. Cajuns — Fiction.]
I. Smith, Cat Bowman, ill.   II. Title.
PZ7.T36967Fg   1998
[E] — dc20   96-14193

10 9 8 7 6 5 4 3 2 1

SC

Published simultaneously in Canada by Little, Brown & Company (Canada) Limited

Printed in Hong Kong

Author's Note

What exactly is a Cajun? Well, Cajun people are natives of southern Louisiana. Their ancestors were exiled from Acadia, Canada, during the 1700s (the term *Cajun* comes from the word *Acadia*). This part of Canada had been a French colony, but when it was taken over by the British, the Acadians, who were proudly French, refused to take an oath of loyalty to the British crown and refused to take up arms against other Frenchmen. They were cruelly driven from the colony. Every male ten years of age and older was forced onto a ship and then transported down the eastern coast of North America. Husbands were separated from their wives; children were separated from their parents. Very few Cajuns survived the ordeal. Those who *did* made their way to the French settlements of Louisiana and finally found peace in the isolated southern swamps. They were able to live off the land by fishing, trapping, and fur trading, much as they had in Acadia.

The Cajun culture is rich and unique and has remained relatively unchanged across the course of time. Cajun cooking features unusual catch found in the bayou, like crawfish, catfish, frog's legs, and alligator, blended in tasty sauces with hot spices. Music is an important part of Cajun life, too. Their special mix of instruments such as the accordion and fiddle creates lively rhythms that invite dancing along. Their language is a unique combination of French and quirky twists of English phrases, spoken with a distinctive accent. Why, there's nothing Cajun people like better than telling a good joke or a tall tale. In fact, *this* tale revolves around the Cajun legend about the *loup garou* (loo guh-ROO).

What exactly is a *loup garou?* The term literally means "werewolf" in French. According to Cajun folklore, the *loup garou* is a creature who is part man, part wolf, who lives deep in the swamp and comes out when the moon is full. Tale has it that his favorite dinner is a smart-alecky boy or a disobedient girl. Is the *loup garou* real? Perhaps in our *minds,* and in stories like *this* one. But if you mind your loved ones, the *loup garou* shouldn't worry you at all. In fact, snuggle up to a loved one right now, and "pass a good time" reading this Cajun tall tale . . . ya hear?

A Cajun Glossary and Pronunciation Guide

The dialogue in this book is written as it would sound in Cajun country. You can use the pronunciation guide below and the Recipe for a Cajun Accent on the back cover to help you read the story like a true Cajun!

Albert (al-BARE)

beaucoup (boh-KOO)
French for *a lot*

chère (shaa, with an *a* as in *cat*)
French for *dear;* used by Cajuns, with their own distinctive pronunciation, as a term of endearment

crabbing
When Cajuns go crabbing, they try to lure a crab out of its mud hole with a piece of bacon or other bait tied to the end of a string.

fais do-do (fay doh-doh)
The French term literally means to "make sleep," but in the Cajun culture, a *fais do-do* is a big party where dancing and festivities last long into the night. Babies sleep in a back room so their parents don't have to leave early.

Feliciana Feydra LeRoux
(fuh-lee-see-AH-nah FAY-druh luh-ROO)

jambalaya (jom-bah-LIE-yah)
A rice dish with sausage, chicken, and seafood

jeune fille (joon fee; with a soft *j* sound, as in *rouge*)
French for *young girl*

Loup Garou (loo guh-ROO)
Literally French for *werewolf*

mais (may)
French for *but*

Memère (m'MARE)
Mother, from the French for *my mother*

Monsieur (m'SYUH)
French for *Mister*

Octave (awk-TAVE)

oui (wee)
French for *yes*

pralines (prah-LEENZ)
Very sweet brown sugar candies made with pecans

Renee (ruh-NAY)

sassafrass
A flavorful spice, but in this case, Memère means Feliciana's being "sassy"

ti (tee)
From the French *petit,* meaning *little;* used as a Cajun prefix, as in *ti-Jacques,* to mean *Jr.*

ti-Jacques (tee-JAHK; with a soft *j* sound, as in *rouge*)

ti-Jean (tee-JAWn; with a soft *j* sound, as in *rouge*)

ti-Juste (tee-JOOST; with a soft *j* sound, as in *rouge*)

Feliciana Feydra LeRoux was in a snit,
and she just couldn't work herself out of it no matter how
hard she tried.
"Hooo! You're crankier than a soft-shell crab!" said Octave.
Go 'way an' leave me alone," retorted Feliciana, tossing
her pigtails.

It started from the time she woke up
and lasted throughout the day.
She turned her nose up at breakfast;

she took a sassy tone with Grampa Baby;
she squirmed and fussed while
Memère brushed out her hair.

She went crabbing with the boys — of
course, they didn't want her to go —
and *everyone* caught crabs *beaucoup*
— especially ti-Jacques,
who caught twelve —
but she couldn't lure *one* from its hole.

"Think you're so great," muttered Feliciana. "If I'da caught some, I'da hung 'em from my ears like earrings."
H'well, not only did ti-Jacques let two crabs dangle from his earlobes, but he *also* attached one to his nose. You could tell by the way his eyes watered and winced that those crab claws were pinching tight!

"Now — top dat! I *dare* ya!" ti-Jacques declared.
Then he twirled Feliciana's pigtails in the air and said, "Go do what girls do *best* — go fix ya'hair or somethin'!"

Feliciana's face was redder than a boiled crawfish!
She stormed home with her brothers trailing behind her;
then she marched straight to the place where Memère kept her
good scissors, and in one whack, her pigtail fell to the floor as her brothers
watched in stunned silence.
"There! I *fixed* my hair!"

"Hoooo," laughed ti-Jacques, doubling over, "you gonna get it now! You been so bad today, d'Loup Garou's gonna come lookin' fo' you."

"Phooey on d'Loup Garou," sniffed Feliciana, beginning to realize just how bad she'd been. "Y'all just made 'im up to scare me."

Since the beginning of time, Feliciana's brothers had told horrible tales by candlelight about the Loup Garou and about the things he'd do to children who misbehaved.

An awe came over their voices when they spoke of him, like they were describing the pope of the swamps.

"He stands seven foots tall
on 'is hind legs," said Albert.

"Seven an' a *half*,"
corrected Octave.

"He's the meanest, most vicious werewolf
you'd never wanna see! Part wolf, part man,
part monster," said ti-Jean, "with teeth sharper
than a gator's, an' breath worsuh-smellin' than a
dead armadillo!"

"An' he eats bad li'l girls an' boys," whispered ti-Juste.
"From d'tip o' dey hair to dey baby toenails," added Renee.

Oh, the boys could paint a frightening picture, yeah.
But right now, Feliciana was way more worried about *Memère* than the
Loup Garou.

At first, Feliciana tried to hide what she'd done under her hat.
But ti-Jacques picked her hat off her head, and when Memère saw Feliciana,
she screamed like she'd seen her dead granny's ghost!

"FELICIANA FEYDRA LEROUX! YO' BEAUTIFUL HAIR!"
"Ti-Jacques *made* me do it!" said Feliciana.
"Did not!" chimed ti-Jacques.

"How can anyone *make* you cut y'own hair?"demanded Memère.
"But — he *did!*"
"Don't *but* me, Miss Sassafrass! You've been fouler than a chicken all day.
You' definitely not fit fo' human company, so you can stay at home tonight while d'rest o' d'family goes to d'*fais do-do!*"

A gasp escaped from all the LeRouxs in the room.
Forbidden to go to d'*fais do-do?!*

Not able to dance and stay up
past your bedtime,
or visit with the whole town and
shoot the breeze?
Not able to taste the jambalaya and sample
the pralines?
Hoooo, Feliciana really snapped the camel's back
this time!

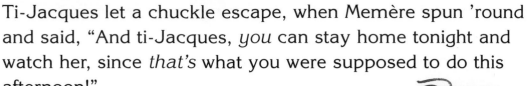

Ti-Jacques let a chuckle escape, when Memère spun 'round and said, "And ti-Jacques, *you* can stay home tonight and watch her, since *that's* what you were supposed to do this afternoon!"

Ti-Jacques swallowed so much air, he almost bust! "Memère, dat's not *fair!* Feliciana's been the toad all day — not me!"

"Maybe if you'd kep' a better eye on yo' baby sistuh, instead of eggin' her on, she'd still have two pigtails, instead of one an' a half."

As evening fell, everyone dressed up in their finest, getting ready for the *fais do-do*. Everyone but ti-Jacques and Feliciana.

The family waved good-bye, promising to bring back a bowl of this or a slice of that.

But the quiet after they left was deafening. Hoooo, it was chilly in the room for August, I'ma *tol'* y'all.

Ti-Jacques glared at Feliciana and said through gritted teeth, "Just you wait, Feliciana Feydra LeRoux. D'Loup Garou's gonna be sniffin' you out like a pork chop, an' I'ma point him right to yo' bed!"

"Dey's no Loup Garou! You jus' pullin' my legs over my eyes," said Feliciana bravely. But ti-Jacques didn't even bother arguing! He walked to his room and slammed the door.

Feliciana gulped, clutching her pecan baby doll, and decided the best thing to do was to climb in bed and make this day *end*. She said a little prayer, hoping her brother could forgive her, and pulled her covers about her neck.

"G'night, ti-Jacques," she called out.
There was no answer.
"I say, g'*night*, ti-Jacques." Nothing.

Try as she might, Feliciana just couldn't get comfortable.
She punched her pillow, she tossed, she flipped, she kicked her twisted
sheets — until a bloodcurdling howl froze her very veins.
"*Ooww — ow-ow-ow!*"
The Loup Garou already had her scent!

Another howl rang out just outside her
window. *"Ow-ow-ooww!"*
She *dove* under the covers and wadded up in a ball,
praying her end would be quick —
when all of a sudden it became perfectly clear!
Ti-Jacques was playing a *trick* on her.
He was the one howling. She *knew* it!
Feliciana threw her covers off and
walked to the window.
"Ha, ha, *ha!* Very funny, ti-Jacques!"
she called out in the darkness.
Not even a breeze broke the stillness
outside.

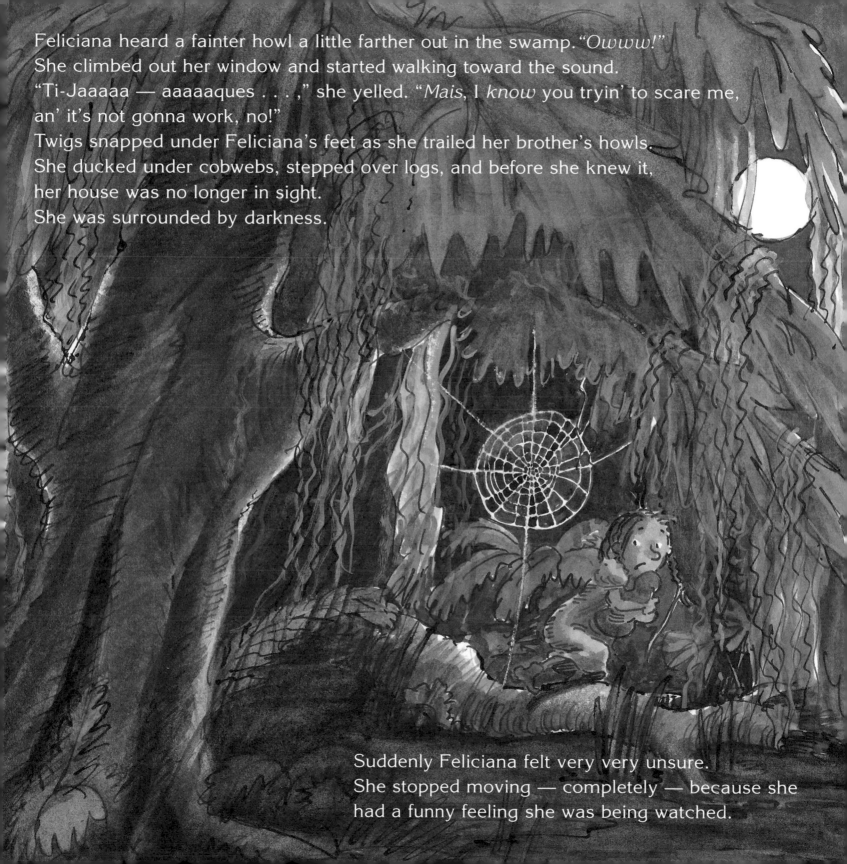

Feliciana heard a fainter howl a little farther out in the swamp. *"Owww!"*
She climbed out her window and started walking toward the sound.
"Ti-Jaaaaa — aaaaaques . . . ," she yelled. "*Mais,* I *know* you tryin' to scare me,
an' it's not gonna work, no!"
Twigs snapped under Feliciana's feet as she trailed her brother's howls.
She ducked under cobwebs, stepped over logs, and before she knew it,
her house was no longer in sight.
She was surrounded by darkness.

Suddenly Feliciana felt very very unsure.
She stopped moving — completely — because she
had a funny feeling she was being watched.

A bone-rattling
"OWW . . . OW-OW-OWWW"
ripped the inky night —
and the fuzz on Feliciana's neck stood straight up.

Faster than you could peel a crawfish, a shadow
crossed Feliciana's face,
and a monstrous creature dropped from the
branches of a tree!
The Loup Garou!

His beady yellow eyes glowed close together like a hawk's.
His matted, knotted hair hung long and tangled like moss,
and when he opened his jaws, flashing his dagger-sharp teeth,
his breath stunk worse than five-day-old fish!

"H'well, well well . . . ," snarled the Loup Garou with a sinister laugh.
"I've had my *eyes* on you, Feliciana Feydra LeRoux."
He slowly circled the child, licking drool from his lips.
"You're gonna taste *sooooo* good — 'cuz you've been *soooooooo* bad!"

Feliciana opened her mouth, but her voice had left town.
Her eyes stretched so wide, they almost popped out on the ground.
She couldn't move.

"Ohhh . . . what's the matter?" the Loup Garou asked in a sugarcane-sweet voice. "Catfish got your tongue?" Then he lunged forward and growled, "Speak UP, *jeune fille!* I DARE ya!" At this, the Loup Garou threw his head back and cackled at his own joke.

"'I *dare* ya!' Oh, that's good! I guess that's all it takes to get *you* huffin' and puffin', an' choppin' off yo' hair — *oui?* After I finish wit' you, I'm gonna sneak back to that LeRoux house an' get dat li'l daredevil ti-Jacques! He'll make a delicious dessert after my MAIN COURSE!"

Now, Feliciana's nerves were so rattled, she was about to pass out cold.
But when the Loup Garou said he was gonna get *ti-Jacques, too,*
the words hit her like a stiff whiff of smelling salts,
and her backbone snapped back in place!
"Now, you hold on a minute," said Feliciana, planting her hands on her hips.
"Who do you think you are, talkin' 'bout eatin' ti-Jacques for dessert!"

The Loup Garou was stunned. *Nobody* had ever talked *back* to him before!
"*Where* are my manners?" said the Loup Garou. "I haven't introduced myself
properly! I'm —"
"I know who you are!" interrupted Feliciana, "an' aren' choo *ashamed* of
yo'self, scarin' li'l chirren, eatin' dey baby toenails. Nasty!" she said,
crossing her arms and wrinkling her nose.
"I see . . . ," said the Loup Garou, leaning closer to her face. "I should be
less of a beast, an' mo' well behaved . . . like *you!*"

The day flashed back before Feliciana's eyes, and there wasn't much to be proud of. She sighed all the way to her toes.

"Look," she said suddenly with her eyes cast down, "my brother hates me, Memère's mad at me, I ruined my hair, I couldn't go to d'*fais do-do* — if you're gonna eat me, just get it over with."

The Loup Garou looked the child over, then sat down next to her and said, "Mmmm. You got problems."

"H'well, dat's what I'm tellin' ya! I was so bad today, I didn't even want to
stop bein' bad!"
"I *know* how dat is!" agreed the Loup Garou.
And the two shared a moment of silence.

"What do *you* do when you' havin' a bad day an' you jus' can't seem to stop it?" asked Feliciana.

"H'why, I howl at d'moon," he said. The Loup Garou cocked his head back and wailed up toward the moss. *"AAAOOWWW!"*

It looked like it felt so good that Feliciana joined in, too, and together they made that moon shake in the sky!

Feliciana and the Loup Garou had a good chuckle over their bad reputations. "Hooo, if my brothers could see me now, they wouldn't believe it! It was worth missin' d'*fais do-do* to meet you, Monsieur Loup Garou." Then she paused. "Dey's just one t'ing I got to ask you. . . . Do you really eat chirren?" The Loup Garou waved his paw. "Shooo! I don't need d'heartburn, *chère*."

The Loup Garou escorted Feliciana back to her window, then said, "Remember, when t'ings get bad, you know what to do." And they shared one last "*Hoow-ow-ow-owl*" at the moon.

Feliciana tiptoed into ti-Jacques's room and whispered in his ear,
"I'm sorry I was such a beas' today."
Ti-Jacques tousled Feliciana's uneven hair, and she knew she was forgiven.

So here's a whisper for *you*. Night-night! Sleep tight. And don't let d'Loup
Garou bite!

ST. JOHN THE BAPTIST PARISH LIBRARY
1334 WEST AIRLINE HIGHWAY
LaPLACE, LOUISIANA 70068